THIS BLOOMSBURY BOOK

BELONGS TO

....

To my daughter Kysha — F.C.

To my son Jamie — M.T.

Bloomsbury Publishing, London, Berlin, New York and Sydney

First printed in Great Britain in 1998 by Bloomsbury Publishing Plc
This Paperback and CD edition first published in September 2005
This paperback edition first published 1999

Text copyright © Faustin Charles 1998
Illustrations copyright © Michael Terry 1998
The moral right of the author and illustrator has been asserted

A CIP catalogue record for this book is available from the British Library
ISBN 978 0 7475 4193 6 (paperback)

28

ISBN 978 0 7475 8113 0 (paperback and CD)

12

Designed by Dawn Apperley
Printed and bound by South China Printing Company, Dongguan City, Guangdong

All papers used by Bloomsbury Publishing are natural, recyclable products made
from wood grown in well-managed forests. The manufacturing processes conform to
the environmental regulations of the country of origin

www.bloomsbury.com/childrens

THE SELFISH CROCODILE

Faustin Charles and Michael Terry

BLOOMSBURY

LONDON BERLIN NEW YORK SYDNEY

Deep in the forest, in the river, lived a large crocodile. He was a very selfish crocodile. He didn't want any other creature to drink or bathe in the river. He thought it was HIS river.

Every day, he shouted to the creatures of the forest, 'Stay away from my river! It's MY river! If you come in my river, I'll eat you all!'

So there were no fish, no tadpoles, no frogs, no crabs, no crayfish in the river. All were afraid of the selfish crocodile.

The forest creatures kept away from the river as well.
Whenever they were thirsty, they went for miles to drink in
other rivers and streams.

Every day the crocodile lay on his great big back in the sun, picking his big, sharp teeth with a stick.

But early one morning, the forest was awakened by a loud groaning sound. Something was in terrible pain.

The creatures thought that it was an animal caught by the crocodile.

GROAN

But as the sun came out brightly, they saw that it was the crocodile who was in pain. He was lying on his big back, holding his swollen jaw, and he was crying real tears.

GROAN

The creatures drew closer – but not too close. Some of the creatures felt sorry for the crocodile.

'What's the matter with him?' asked a deer.

'I don't know,' said a squirrel.

'Maybe he's going to die,' chirped a bird.

'If that happens it'll be safe to go in the river!' grunted a wild pig.

The animals thought about this. They hung from branches, they hung from vines; they buzzed in the air, and they shook their heads as they watched the great big crocodile in pain. No animal tried to help.

Suddenly a little mouse appeared, sniffing the air.
He ran along the crocodile's tail, then on to his tummy.
The other creatures stared.

'Look at that mouse!' chattered a monkey.

'He's either very brave or mad!'

'He's going to be eaten for sure!' said an iguana.

The mouse crept along the crocodile's big neck, and into his open mouth.

There was a hush in the forest.

The mouse got hold of something, and pulled and pulled and pulled. Then he put it on his shoulder and walked out of the crocodile's mouth.

There was a loud cheer from the astonished creatures.

The crocodile sat up and said, 'I don't feel any more pain. It's all gone!'

Then he saw the mouse walking down his tummy, carrying an enormous crocodile tooth on his shoulder.

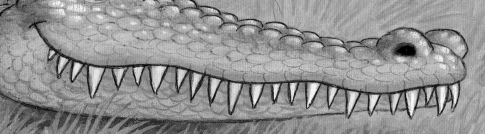

'Your bad tooth was giving you the tooth-ache!'
answered the mouse, turning around to face the
now-smiling crocodile. 'Do you want it back?'
'Oh no, no, no, get rid of it, and when you've done that,

come back, I'll have a present for you.'

The mouse went and buried the bad tooth under a tree, and when he returned, the crocodile had a nice juicy nut waiting for him.

As the crocodile watched the mouse eating the nut, he said to him, 'You were very clever, getting rid of my tooth-ache – and kind too. I am so grateful. But what shall I do if my tooth-ache comes back?'

'Don't worry, I'll help you take care of your teeth,' answered the mouse, nibbling.

Soon the crocodile and the mouse were the best of friends.

And one day the crocodile sent all the animals an invitation.
'Please come to drink and bathe in the river! I won't hurt you!
The river belongs to us all!' he said.

The creatures weren't afraid to drink and bathe in the river any more. Although the crocodile was sometimes snappy, they grew to love him.

And soon the river was full of fish and tadpoles and crabs and crayfish.